Kinds of Grains

by Sara E. Hoffmann

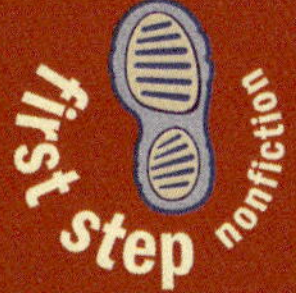

Lerner Publications Company · Minneapolis

I eat oats.

I eat rice.

I eat barley.

I eat popcorn.

All of these are grains.

Grains taste good!

The images in this book are used with the permission of: © Photoeuphoria/Dreamstime.com, p. 2; © Todd Strand/Independent Picture Service, pp. 3, 4; © iStockphoto.com/Kim Gunkel, p. 5; © imagebroker.net/SuperStock, p. 6; © iStockphoto.com/wavebreakmedia, p. 7.

Front cover: © Hong Chan/Dreamstime.com.

Main body text set in ITC Avant Garde Gothic Std Medium 21/25.
Typeface provided by Adobe Systems.

Lerner Publications Company
A division of Lerner Publishing Group, Inc.
241 First Avenue North
Minneapolis, MN 55401 U.S.A.

Website address: www.lernerbooks.com

Library of Congress Cataloging-in-Publication Data

Hoffmann, Sara.
Kinds of grains / by Sara E. Hoffmann.
p. cm. — (First step nonfiction—Kinds of plants)
ISBN 978–1–4677–0498–4 (pbk. : alk. paper)
1. Grain—Juvenile literature. I. Title.
SB189.H69 2013
633.1—dc23 2012002934

Manufactured in the United States of America
2 - 44709 - 12878 - 3/8/2022